LUCKY DUCKY

Doreen Mulryan

Abrams Books for Young Readers
New York

Library of Congress Cataloging-in-Publication Data

Mulryan, Doreen, author, illustrator.
Lucky Ducky / by Doreen Mulryan.
pages cm
Summary: "Ducky is unlucky. Somehow things always turn out wrong for him.
One day he decides to go to the park to look for a four-leaf clover, which
he knows will bring him good luck. But instead of finding a four-leaf clover,
he meets Piggy, then Bunny, then Pup, and he realizes that having fun
with friends makes him the luckiest duck of all"—Provided by publisher.
ISBN 978-1-4197-1467-2
[1. Luck—Fiction. 2. Friendship—Fiction. 3. Ducks—Fiction.
4. Animals—Fiction.] I. Title.
PZ7.M9228Lu 2016
[E]—dc23
2015016394

Text and illustrations copyright © 2016 Doreen Mulryan
Book design by Pamela Notarantonio

Printed and bound in U.S.A.
11 10 9 8 7 6 5 4 3 2

Abrams Books for Young Readers are available at special discounts when purchased
in quantity for premiums and promotions as well as fundraising or educational
use. Special editions can also be created to specification. For details, contact
specialsales@abramsbooks.com or the address below.

THE ART OF BOOKS SINCE 1949
115 West 18th Street
New York, NY 10011
www.abramsbooks.com

Thank you to
all of my family and friends
for your love and support.
You make me feel lucky
every day!

Doreen

This is **Ducky**.

He thinks he's **unlucky**.

No matter how
hard he tries,

things just don't seem
to come out right.

But Ducky doesn't let his tough luck get him down.

Ducky decides to go to the park
to find a four-leaf clover.

That should do the trick!

Ducky has so much fun playing Frisbee

that he forgets to look for a four-leaf clover.

Ducky starts to look for
a four-leaf clover again,
but then . . .

Join me for
a swim?

Ducky loves swimming and splashing!

But if I want to be lucky, I need to go back to my search.

Ducky tries looking for a four-leaf clover once more, but then...

Ducky doesn't find a four-leaf clover.

But he realizes that he's found much more.

This is
DUCKY.

He knows he's
LUCKY.

Because no matter what happens . . .

. . . as long as he has friends . . .

He's the luckiest
duck of all!